TIME TO SLEEP

For Aunt Opal

ISBN 0-590-63607-3

Copyright © 1997 by Denise Fleming.
All rights reserved. Published by Scholastic Inc., 555 Broadway, New York, NY 10012, by arrangement with Henry Holt and Company, Inc.

SCHOLASTIC and associated logos are trademarks and/or registered trademarks of Scholastic Inc.

12 11 10 9 8 7 6 5 4 3 2 1   8 9/9 0 1 2 3/0

Printed in the U.S.A.   08

First Scholastic printing, September 1998

The artist used colored cotton rag fiber to create the illustrations for this book.

SCHOLASTIC INC.
New York Toronto London Auckland Sydney

TIME TO SLEEP

DENISE FLEMING

Bear sniffed once.
She sniffed twice.
"I smell winter in the air,"
said Bear.
"It is time to crawl
into my cave and sleep.
But first I must tell Snail."

Snail was slowly slithering
up one leaf and down another.
"Snail," rumbled Bear,
"winter is in the air.
It is time to seal
your shell and sleep."

Snail stopped slithering.
"You are right, Bear," said Snail.
"This morning there was frost on the grass.
It is time to sleep.
But first I must tell Skunk."

Scritch, scratch, scratch.
Skunk was busy digging grubs.
"Skunk, winter is on its way,"
said Snail. "It is time for you
to curl up in your den and sleep."

Skunk looked up.
The leaves on the trees were yellow and red.
"All right," said Skunk, "I will sleep.
But first I must tell Turtle."

Turtle was off on a ramble.

"Stop, Turtle!" cried Skunk.

"I have news. Winter is on its way."

Turtle blinked. "Winter?"

"Yes, winter," said Skunk.

"It is time for you to dig down deep and sleep."

"The days have been growing shorter,"
muttered Turtle. "It is time to sleep.
But first I must tell Woodchuck."

Turtle trudged up Woodchuck's hill.
"Woodchuck," called Turtle, "winter is on its way.
It is time for you to burrow down and sleep."

"Thank goodness," said Woodchuck, with a sigh. "My skin is so tight I could not eat another bite. I am ready to sleep. But first I must tell Ladybug."

Ladybug was perched
high on a branch in a maple tree.
"Ladybug," called Woodchuck,
"winter is on its way."

Ladybug flew over Woodchuck's head.
"The leaves are falling from the trees,"
said Woodchuck.
"It is time for you to slip under a log and sleep."
"All right," said Ladybug.
"But first I must tell Bear."

Bear was softly snoring in her cave.
"Bear!" cried Ladybug.
"Wake up! Wake up!"
Bear grumbled and rolled over.
"The sky is full of geese
honking good-bye," cried Ladybug.
"Winter is on its way, Bear."

Bear opened one eye.
Then she opened the other eye.
"What?" growled Bear.
"It is time to crawl into your cave and sleep,"
said Ladybug.
"Ladybug," grumbled Bear, "I *am* in my cave.
I *was* asleep."
"Oh dear," said Ladybug, "I am so sorry, Bear.
Please go back to sleep."

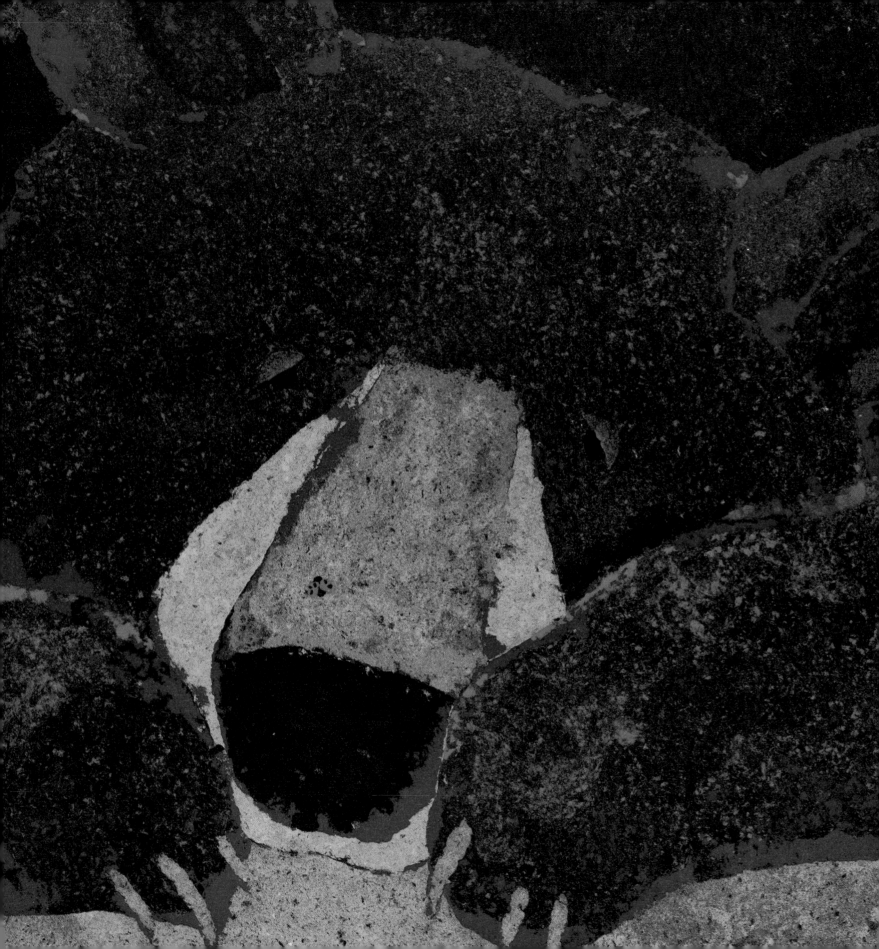

Bear rolled over and closed her eyes.
Ladybug slipped under a log nearby.

"Good night, Bug,"
said Bear.

"Good night, Bear," said Ladybug.

"Good night, Woodchuck."

"Good night, Turtle."

"Good night, Skunk."

"Good night, Snail."

"Good night, everyone,

see you in the spring."